For David Davies

First published 1985 by Walker Books Ltd,
87 Vauxhall Walk, London SE11 5HJ

This edition published 2000

2 4 6 8 10 9 7 5 3 1

© 1985 Shirley Hughes

This book has been typeset in Vendome.

Printed in Hong Kong

British Library Cataloguing in Publication Data
A catalogue record for this book is
available from the British Library.

ISBN 0-7445-6737-8 (hb)
ISBN 0-7445-6985-0 (pb)

When We Went to the Park

Shirley Hughes

WALKER BOOKS
AND SUBSIDIARIES
LONDON · BOSTON · SYDNEY

When Grandpa and I
put on our coats

and went

to the park ...

We saw one black cat

sitting on a wall,

Two big girls
licking ice-creams,

Three ladies chatting
on a bench,

Four babies
in buggies,

Five children playing
in the sand-pit,

Six runners running,

Seven dogs chasing one another,

Eight boys
kicking a ball,

Nine ducks
swimming on the pond,

Ten birds swooping
in the sky,

and so many leaves that I
couldn't count them all.

On the way back we saw
the black cat again.

Then we went
home for tea.